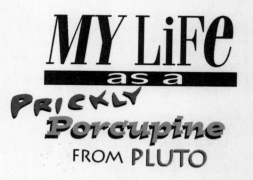

MY LiFe
as a
PRICKLY
Porcupine
FROM PLUTO

the incredible worlds of **Wally McDoogle**

MY LiFe
as a
PRICKLY Porcupine
FROM PLUTO

BILL MYERS

Tommy NELSON®

www.tommynelson.com

A Division of Thomas Nelson, Inc.
www.ThomasNelson.com

Published in Nashville, Tennessee, by Tommy Nelson®, a Division of Thomas Nelson, Inc. Visit us on the Web at www.tommynelson.com.

Verses marked (TLB) are from The Living Bible. Copyright © 1971. Used by permission of Tyndale House Publishers, Inc., Wheaton, Illinois 60189. All rights reserved.

Library of Congress Cataloging-in-Publication Data

Myers, Bill, 1953–
     My life as a prickly porcupine from Pluto / Bill Myers.
        p. cm. — (The incredible worlds of Wally McDoogle ; 23)
     Summary: After he is mistaken for an alien and then kidnapped by revolutionists, bungling Wally McDoogle learns that cheating doesn't pay and that honesty is the best policy.
     ISBN 1-4003-0984-0 (pbk.)
     [1. Cheating—Fiction. 2. Christian life—Fiction.
3. Humorous stories.] I. Title.
     PZ7.M98234Mysq 2004
     [Fic]—dc22

                                              2004003155

Printed in the United States of America
06 07 08 WRZ 8 7 6

For Skip Ball:
A man committed to honesty.

"The Lord hates cheating and delights in honesty."

—Proverbs 11:1 (TLB)

Contents

Ever notice there are exactly the same number of letters in the word *C H E A T* as there are in the word *W R O N G*?

Coincidence? I don't think so.

(Though it is a *complete coincidence* that there are the same number of letters in *D I S A S T E R* as in *M c D O O G L E* . . . and in *W A L L Y* as in *M O R O N* and *I D I O T* and *L O S E R* and . . . well, you get the picture.)

Unfortunately, I didn't . . . until it was too late.

Lots of people cheat. Right?

Right.

And if everybody's doing it, it must be okay. Right?

WRONG!

(Sorry, didn't mean to yell.)

BUT IT *REALLY* IS!
(Guess you can tell it's kind of a touchy subject.)

Anyway, it all started Sunday night. Everybody in the ol' family unit was doing what they do best:

- Dad was lying on the sofa examining the inside of his eyelids.
- Burt (or was it Brock? I can never keep my twin brothers straight.) was busy wrecking the family car. (Hey, everybody needs a hobby.)
- Brock (or was it Burt?) was working in the garage on a weird science project with a bunch of porcupine quills he got from some catalog.
- Mom was in the kitchen teaching little sister Carrie how to avoid poisoning the entire family with her charcoal-burgers.

And me? I was busy bruising my brain over tomorrow's science test on the solar system. That is, until . . .

Warning, Wally. Warning, Wally.
Warning, Wally. Warning, Wally.

That, of course, is the special ring I've pro-grammed into my cell phone to let me know when it's Wall Street calling.

Of course, a smarter person wouldn't pick up. Which, of course, is why I did.

"Hello?"

"Hey, Wally," she said. "Great news!"

"You've quit trying to make your first million bucks off me?"

"Get real," she said.

"Everybody has a dream." I sighed.

"I just found out what's going to be on tomor-row's science test. Want to know?"

Of course, asking for that type of info is a major no-no. It would mean becoming, like, a major cheat. So I took a stand, cleared my throat, and firmly said: "Um, er, uh, I don't, um, uh—"

"Right," she said, obviously figuring my indecision was a decision. "What we have to do is write an essay on our favorite planet."

"Wall Street—"

"Don't thank me now. You can pay me back later."

"Pay you back?"

"Just $19.95 a month for the rest of your life—or until you die, whichever comes first."

"But—"

"See ya."

"Wall Street, I don't—"

Click

So there I was with info hotter than a boiling kettle on a stove on the sun . . . in July. What should I do? What would you do?

To cheat or not to cheat, that is the question.

Should I study as planned . . . or cheat by hitting the ol' Internet and loading up with info on my favorite planet?

I wanted to do the right thing, but for some reason, my fingers didn't. And before you could say, "Buckle in, here we go again," my plump pinkies turned on the computer and typed:

P L U T O
(Bad fingers! Bad fingers!)

Unfortunately, this was also about the time I reached over and took a guilty gulp of soda. No problem, except for the part where I accidentally spilled the entire can over the entire

K-Zap, K-Crackle, K-Pop

keyboard.

Being an expert at such clumsiness, I immediately wiped off the keyboard with my T-shirt (what else are T-shirts for?), only to discover that I'd accidentally logged on to some government Web site about Pluto.

Soon I was sitting in front of the screen, memorizing all sorts of cool stuff. Some of it was pretty weird, but it didn't matter.

The good news was, my test grade would be incredibly great.

The bad news was, my life would be incredibly not.

Sure, I knew I was cheating, but it's not like anybody was getting hurt.

Unfortunately, I couldn't have been more wrong. Somebody was getting hurt.

AND THAT SOMEBODY WAS ME!
(Sorry.)

* * * * *

A couple of hours later I lay in bed, almost sound asleep (except for the part about being wide awake). I'm not sure why. Maybe it had something to do with all the information from the Web site running around in my head (or all the guilt running around in my heart).

Whatever the reason, I figured I'd break out Ol' Betsy, my laptop computer, and drown my thoughts in another one of my superhero stories.

It was another incredibly imaginative and intensely interesting day for Invento Man McDoogle. Already he and his stupendously smart and super spiffy staff had created:

- AN AUTOMATIC SOCKS PICKER-UPPER. Tired of Mom always telling you to pick up your socks? This little machine will do it all by itself. (Though there's still some problems with its mistaking your pet hamster for your white gym socks.)

- A SPEECH SUM-UPPER. One press of the remote-control button and all those long-winded politicians (and teachers) get to the point of their speech in 2.3 seconds (8.6 seconds in Texas).

- A REMOTE-CONTROLLED NOSE PICKER. (Don't even ask.)

Invento Man is just about to break for lunch when suddenly the Villain Alarm begins to

BAD GUY ALERT, BAD GUY ALERT

sound.

Quicker than you can say, "Uh-oh, here we go again," our hero checks the security monitor. His entire Invento Staff is down in the Invento Lab. But, instead of inventing gonzo-gizmos and cool contraptions, they're just sitting around on the sofa and, horror of horrors...

(insert scary music here)

watching TV!

That's right. Instead of inventing imaginative items or pondering ponderously perplexing problems, they're thinking of...nothing.

In a flash of genius, our superhero hits the intercom button and shouts: "Hey guys...what's up?"

No answer. Just empty faces staring at an even emptier TV show.

"Uh, guys...you promised you'd have the solution to world hunger by noon."

Nothing but more emptiness.

"And a cure for cancer by five o'clock."

Nothing but more nothing. Until, suddenly, another face comes onto the monitor. The fiendishly foul features of

Ta-Da-DAAAA...

(That, of course, is the bad-guy music.)

Couch Potato Dude!

"Couch Potato Dude!" our hero cries. "Is that you?"

"Of course. Didn't you just hear the music?"

"Oh, yeah."

"And isn't it Tuesday?"

"Oh, yeah, again."

"And you know Tuesdays are my day for attempted world domination."

(I hope you, dear reader, are paying attention, 'cause there's definitely going to be a test.)

"What are you doing this time?"

Invento Man sighs. "Slipping Brain-Numbing Solution into the water supply again?"

"Been there, done that."

"Removing all human thought with your BRAIN-DELETE button?"

"Please, that is so-o-o-o two super-hero stories ago. No, I've got something way better."

"Oh, no."

"Oh, yes. It's my greatest invention of all. Could I have some more bad-guy music, please?"

Ta-Da-DAAAA. . .

"A little louder."

Ta-Da-DAAAA. . .

"Thank you. It's my latest invention, and I call it. . ."

Ta-Da-DAAAA. . .

"Right, I think they've got the idea. It's my latest invention, and I call it. . .TV!"

"TV?!" Our hero smirks. "All that introduction music just for TV?"

"That's right."

"But TV's already been invented."

"It has?"

"Of course."

"Ah, but not with mindless sitcom TV shows."

"Afraid so."

"What about mindless cartoons?"

"Sorry."

"But what about dumb dramas where you sit around and watch other people live exciting lives so you don't have time to live your own exciting life?"

"Sorry, Couch Potato Dude, they've been doing that for years."

"Oh, great...." Our bad guy groans. "I suppose they've also got the special beam that I've built into the sets to hypnotize people to make them watch."

"Well, uh, actually"—Invento Man clears his throat—"that would be new."

"Great! Then that's what the music was for!"

"But you can't do that to people!" our hero shouts.

"Can and did. Just look at your Invento Staff."

The monitor flashes back to his Invento Crew as they sit around on their sofa, watching TV.

"Hey, guys," our hero shouts.

Nothing.

"Guys, we've got way cooler things to do than just sitting around."

More in the nothing department.

"What have you done to my staff?!" Invento Man cries.

"Not just your staff." Couch Potato sneers. "The entire world. Soon everybody will be in my clutches. Soon no one will have a life. All they'll do is sit around and watch and watch and—"

"Wally?"

"—watch and watch and—"

"Wally McDoogle, answer me!" It was Mom calling from down the hall. "Are you still on that computer?"

"No, Mom. I'm sound asleep."

"You turn it off right now, young man. It's way past your bedtime."

"Oh, all right." Reluctantly, I hit SAVE and shut Ol' Betsy down. I'd get back to Couch Potato and Invento Man a little later. Right now, it was time to get some rest. Tomorrow was going to be a very big day.

Unfortunately, I had no idea just how big *"very big"* would be. . . .

Chapter 2

Cheater!

So there I was sinning, er, I mean *sitting* in Reptile Man's science class. Actually, his real name is Mr. Reptenson, and he's nice enough, except . . . well, I don't want to say he spits when he talks, but after the third or fourth day, we all wised up and started wearing raincoats. (Except for the kids in the first row, who started bringing umbrellas . . . and diver's masks . . . with snorkels.)

So there I was sitting and sinning, er, sitting and *staring* at the one and only science question on our test:

Write a paragraph about your favorite planet.

Yes sir, it was just like Wall Street had said. Now all I had to do was decide what to do. Once again the question rose in my head . . .

To cheat or not to cheat, that is the question.
Unfortunately, it's a question that only took
1.3 seconds to answer. Especially since:

1. Science is my worst class. (Next to math, English, geography, social studies, spelling, and, of course, P.E.)
2. I'd agreed to pay my best friend $19.95 a month for the rest of my life (or until my death, whichever comes first).
3. I'm writing this book about all the awful stuff that happens when someone with incredible unintelligence cheats.

So, not being the brightest light bulb in the package, I sat, stared, and began sinning—no, no, no, why do I keep saying that?! I sat, stared, and began *scrawling* out the information I'd memorized from the secret government Web site.

Sure, I could have been honest and not cheated. Sure, I could have written about another planet. But that would have gone against my McDoogle Lifetime Motto:

When in Doubt, Mess Up
(Hey, everybody needs a code to live by.)

Did I feel bad? Not really.

Not even when I finished, took my paper up front, and did my usual . . .

K-trip
K-fall
K-thud.
(Sometimes I'm a little clumsy when I'm nervous.)

"Hey, Wally," Reptile Man asked as he helped me back to my feet, "are you okay? You look a little nervoussss."

I ducked his saliva shower and cried, "Sinning?! Who's sinning?!"

He looked at me kinda funny. "I didn't ssssay anything about sssssinning."

"Oh," I said, reaching down to ring out my shirt. (It was drenched in either sweat or saliva . . . or both.) "'Cause I'm really not sinning— well, unless you count the lie I'm telling you now about not sinning, which, of course, would mean I'm sinning by telling you that I'm not, 'cause I am, uh, er. . . ."

Reptile Man's puzzled look slowed me to a stop. "Sssssorry?" he asked.

I tried to answer, but suddenly my mouth was dryer than a cotton ball under a hair dryer on top of a heat vent in the middle of Death Valley. So I only nodded.

"Well, okay, then," he said. "Have a sssssu-per nicccccce day."

I smiled, wiped my face, and turned to leave.

Did I feel bad about cheating? Not yet. The way I figured, I'd have plenty of time to be feeling bad. (With eight chapters to go in this book, I'd have *more* than plenty of time.)

* * * * *

The rest of my day was pretty normal. You know, just the usual, run-of-the-mill:

- Tripping and nosediving down the school steps. (I've tried belly-flopping and, though the *PLOP!* noise is a lot cooler, you just don't break as many bones that way.) This, of course, was followed by:

- The required visit to the Emergency Room to reset those broken bones and replace any and all destroyed organs. (Don't worry about the cost; Dad got me a season pass.) And, finally, we end with:

- The joyful celebration of my classmates when I return, which also involves the usual eighth-grade bullies grabbing me, turning me upside down, sticking my head in the toilet, and flushing it. (I just love class reunions, don't you?)

Unfortunately, my evening wasn't quite so peaceful. . . .

I first began to suspect there might be a problem when an entire fleet of helicopters began

*WHOP WHOP WHOP WHOPP*ing

directly over our house.

My second clue was when I raced to look out my bedroom window and saw a dozen army tanks arriving on our front lawn.

Being the curious type, I threw open my window and shouted, "Hey, what's going on?"

I was greeted by giant searchlights blasting on and blazing into my eyes.

But what really made me think there might be a problem was when some voice shouted up at me through a bullhorn:

"THIS IS THE F.I.B.—THROW DOWN YOUR RAY GUN AND COME OUT WITH YOUR TENTACLES UP!"

I shaded my eyes from the lights and calmly screamed, "What are you talking about?!"

"DON'T PLAY STUPID WITH US!"

"Who's playing? I'm Wally McDoogle. I'm always this way!"

"YOU'RE NOT FOOLING ANYONE WITH THAT CLUMSY GOOFBALL DISGUISE!"

"What disguise?!"

Suddenly, my cell phone rang. I reached into my pocket, pulled it out, and answered, "Hello?"

"Hey, *crunch, crunch,* Wally."

It was Opera, my other best friend, the human eating machine. He's a major junk-food junkie. You name it, he'll eat it. Potato chips, corn chips, asparagus chips—it makes no difference; if it's deep-fried, covered in salt, and goes *crunch* or *munch,* it's usually inside his mouth.

"I didn't know you were an, *munch, munch,* outer-space alien," he said.

"What?"

"Yeah. I'm watching you live right now on *I-Witless News.*"

"WHAT?"

"They say you blew your cover and, *crunch, munch,* exposed your true identity when you wrote all that top-secret stuff on this afternoon's science test."

"WHAT?!"

"Can you say something else, please? That response is getting a little boring."

"Sorry. How 'bout: EXPOSED MY TRUE IDENTITY?!"

"That's better. Yeah, they say you wrote things about Pluto that only top scientists or outer-space aliens would, *munch, crunch,* know. And since you're not exactly a whiz at science, they figured out that you were really an—"

"Opera, I'm no alien!"

"It's okay, Wally. I'm not prejudiced . . . as long as you don't, *burp,* neutralize me with your ray gun."

"I don't have a—"

"Of course you do. It's all over the news, and we know the news never, *belch,* lies."

"Opera!?"

The voice from the bullhorn interrupted: "IF YOU DON'T COME OUT, THEN WE'RE COMING IN AFTER YOU!"

I looked out the window. Don't get me wrong, I like being the center of attention as much as the next guy. But there was something about a thousand National Guardsmen with a thousand National Guard rifles all pointed at me (not to mention those dozen tanks with their dozen cannons) that suddenly made me a little camera shy. So I stepped out of the light and flattened myself against the wall.

"Opera," I whispered into the phone. "You've got to get me out of here."

And, being the true-blue friend that he is, thinking only about me and my tremendous problem, he asked, "Do they have potato chips on Pluto?"

"I am not a space invader!!"

Suddenly, we were interrupted by a high-pitched

SQUEEEEAAL

that came out of the phone.

"Hello, Opera?" I yelled. "Opera, can you hear me?!"

The voice below shouted:

"WE HAVE JAMMED ALL FREQUENCIES SO YOU CANNOT CONTACT YOUR MOTHER SHIP!"

What was I to do? I could turn myself in and tell the truth. But why should they believe me? If I was dishonest by cheating, why would they think I'm being honest now?

"WE'RE GIVING YOU TO THE COUNT OF TEN."

What should I do?!

"AND IF YOU DON'T COME OUT, YOU'LL NOT ONLY MAKE ME CRANKY . . . BUT

WE'LL ALSO HAVE TO ANNIHILATE YOU
AND YOUR ENTIRE HOUSE!"

Should I make a run for it?

"ONE . . . TWO . . ."

Or should I turn myself in?

"HOLD IT. I'M SORRY . . ."

I caught my breath.

"IT'S ALWAYS MORE DRAMATIC TO
COUNT BACKWARD."

I released my breath.

"TEN . . . NINE . . ."

What to do?

"EIGHT . . . SEVEN . . ."

Tell the truth and be treated like an alien
invader . . .

"SIX . . . FOUR . . ."

Or run to save my life.

"WAIT A MINUTE, THAT'S NOT RIGHT.
LET'S SEE . . . SIX, SIX, DON'T TELL ME,
SIX—OH, YEAH . . . *FIVE* . . . THAT'S RIGHT,
FIVE . . . FOUR . . . UH . . ."

Decisions, decisions . . .

Chapter 3

A Sticky Situation

Fortunately, the guy with the bullhorn was no math whiz. This gave me plenty of time to race downstairs and cry, "Mom, Dad! We've got three seconds before they completely destroy our house!"

That was the good news.

The bad news was, Mom and Dad were both watching the final episode of *Stinking Rich, Perfect-Looking Dude Has to Choose a Perfect-Looking Wife.*

"That's nice," Mom said.

"Grunt," Dad grunted.

"THREE . . . ONE . . . NO, NO, THAT'S NOT RIGHT, DON'T TELL ME . . ."

"You don't understand!" I shouted.

"Please, Sweetheart," Mom said, "we're right in the middle of *Stinking Rich, Perfect-Looking Dude Has to Choose a Perfect-Looking Wife.*"

"But . . ."

"FOUR . . . NO, WAIT, WE ALREADY DID THAT . . . UH . . ."

"Mom!"

"Shhh," Mom shhh-ed.

"THREE . . . YEAH, THAT'S RIGHT . . . THREE . . ."

"Dad!"

"*Grunt,*" Dad grunted.

It was hopeless. So bad that there was nothing I could do but what I had to do, so I went ahead and did it.

TRANSLATION: I turned and raced out the back door for my life!

"There he is!" someone shouted.

As I ran across the backyard toward our garage, all the bright lights swung over to me.

I had two choices—break into a song-and-dance number . . . or keep running for my life.

"It's the invader from Pluto! Blast him! Blow him to smithereens!"

It was a close vote, but the Running For My Life won out.

"Stop him! Don't let him escape! Don't let him escape!"

"OH, GREAT! NOW YOU'VE MADE ME LOSE COUNT. I'LL HAVE TO START ALL OVER. TEN . . . UH . . . NINE . . ."

I arrived at the garage and slipped through
the side door. It was totally dark—well, except
for the gazillion watts of light shining through
the door and windows.

The good news was, this helped me see where
I was going.

The bad news was, it didn't help my coordination.

In fact, I was so blinded that I accidentally
stepped on the rake, which accidentally

*K-Bamb*ed

into my face.

No surprise there. If there's an accident
waiting to happen, I'm just the one to make
sure it does. I wasn't even surprised when I
staggered backward and

*K-Thudd*ed

against the wall, causing all of Mom's hanging
garden tools to

K-boink, K-bonk, K-bunk

onto my head, sending me into the land of semi-
consciousness.

Of course, all of that was child's play—especially for a seasoned catastrophe pro like myself. But what surprised even me was when I staggered forward and fell across the riding lawn mower.

No problem . . . except for the part of getting my belt caught on the "ON" lever and, of course,

cough-cough
chugga-chugga-chugga

firing it up.

And what fun is it to be semiconscious and riding a lawn mower unless your foot accidentally hits the accelerator and you suddenly

VAROOOOM

across the garage at just under the speed of light . . . until you

K-RASH

into the opposite (and very hard) wall?

Now you know why I'm still the champ. Now you know why I am and always will be the World Class, Triple A . . . **Master of Disaster.**

But there was one other sound effect I forgot

to mention. It was kind of faint (which can happen when you're busy losing consciousness), but I clearly remember the

*klug-klug-klug-klugg*ing

of several gallons of glue tipping from a shelf and spilling over my head and other body parts.

Yes sir, it was great to know I hadn't lost the knack. And with that bit of confidence, I figured now was as good a time as any to go completely unconscious.

Still, being unconscious doesn't mean I can't dream. And with my superhero story still running around in the back of my mind, I figured now was as good a time as any to catch up on it . . .

When we last left our hero, Invento Man was getting his undies in a bunch talking to our bad guy over his security monitor. After all, it's not every day some sinisterly slick and slightly sick Couch Potato Dude tries taking over the world.

Just every Tuesday, remember? (I told you there was going to be a test. Now pay attention.)

But our baddest of bad boys is not using chemicals or germs or even that awful radiation that makes your flesh rot. No, dear reader, this is something far worse. This is something that makes your *brain* rot. That's right. This time he is using

Ta-Da-DAAAA...

television.

"And that's just the beginning," the sinisterly sly slime ball snickers. "Soon I'm going to invent hundreds of channels you can choose from with something I'm calling 'Cable.'"

"Uh, Couch Potato Dude, that's already been——"

"And then I'm inventing something called a 'Remote Control,' so you'll never have to get up from your couch to change channels——"

"Uh, Mr. Couch Potato Dude——"

"And best of all, I'm making these incredibly loud and obnoxious things you have to watch called 'gOmercials.'"

"What are they called?" our hero asks.

"GOmercials. They're ways of selling stupid things you really don't need for money you really don't have."

"Oh, you mean COMmercials."

"Com instead of go—Hmmm, I like that. Mind if I use it?"

"It's a free country."

"Not if I have my way. Soon everybody will be slaves to this machine. Families will quit talking to each other."

"But—"

"People will no longer play sports, but just sit around and watch others play them."

"But, but—"

"Kids will no longer use their imaginations. They'll just sit around and let others make up stories."

"But that stuff is already happening!"

"It is?"

"Yes, everything has been invented— well, except for that special beam you mentioned in chapter 1. But if you've forgotten about it, then I shouldn't bring it up because then you'll use it to take over the—"

"Wait a minute, what beam?"

"You remember, the one you built to hypnotize people? Remember, you said that's the only way you can really take over the world?"

"Oh, that's right! I'd almost forgotten! Thanks!"

"Don't mention it. I've been studying for that test our world-famous author mentioned."

"Good for you," the world-famous author writes.

"Thanks," our hero replies. "Say, in the next story can you give me blond hair? I've always liked super-heroes who have——"

"Excuse me," our tyrannical tuber cries. "Can we get back to the story?"

"Sure, but what's a 'tyrannical tuber'?" our hero asks.

"Look it up," Dude whines. "Just let me get to my criminally cool invention."

"Sure."

"Thanks." Couch Potato clears his throat and continues. "All I have to do is activate the Hypno-beam by flipping this switch."

As he speaks, the sinisterly sly supersinner switches a sinisterly sinister and super-sly switch (say that with a mouthful of crackers). The one labeled:

Warning:
Switch only to hypnotize and
control pesky superheroes.

Suddenly, a beam shoots out of Invento Man's monitor.

K-zzz...Zzz...Zzz...Zzz...

And quicker than you can ask, "Wait a minute, how's the good guy supposed to win if he's getting hypnotized?" our hero's eyes glaze over.

Then our baddest of bad boys bellows a boastful

"Boo-hoo-hoo-ha-ha-ha!"

and asks, "What were you saying, Superdud?"

"I, uh, don't, uh...something about stopping you and—"

Couch Potato turns the beam up even

Kzzz...Zzz...Zzz...Zzz...

higher and shouts, "What was that?"

"I, uh...I think I'm just going to sit over on my couch and watch a little TV."

"What about saving the world?"

"Oh, you're right, I better go and—"

Kzzz...Zzz...Zzz...Zzz...

"On second thought, maybe I'll just sit and watch somebody else do that."

"I think that's a nifty keen idea." Couch Potato sneers. "Just sit down, stare at your screen, and let me have all the...

Boo-hoo-hoo-ha-ha-ha!

...fun."

"Yessss..." Invento Man sighs.

"Let me control your imagination."

"Yessss..."

"Let me control the entire world."

"Ye—wait a minute, what about Cleveland?"

Kzzz...Zzz...
Zzz...Zzz...

"Yessss...even Cleveland."

Oh, no! What will Invento Man do?

How will he ever get free of the beam?

How will he ever save the world and Cleveland?

And, more importantly than that importantly, will Couch Potato Dude ever invent a MUTE button for his remote control so we don't have to listen to all those gOmercials?

These were the brilliant, brain-bruising questions bouncing through my muddled mind as I regained consciousness. Then there were the other, more serious ones, like:

1. Why was I lying on top of the riding lawn mower covered in glue?

2. Why did every square inch of my body hurt?

3. What's the capital of South Dakota? (Sorry, but I've always wanted to know.)

And, last but not least . . .

4. What was that weird guy shouting through his bullhorn now?

"THREE . . . TWO . . ."
Suddenly, it all came back to me.
Suddenlier, I wished it hadn't. Because as big a fix as Invento Man was in, it was nothing compared to—
"ONE . . ."
—mine.

Chapter 4

A Prickly Situation

Now, I'm no math genius, but the way I figure it, the guy shouting through the bullhorn was running a little low on numbers.

"ZERO . . ."

Real low.

So, with my magnificent McDoogle courage, I bravely opened my mouth and boldly . . . burst into tears. "Please don't hurt me!" I screamed. "Please, please, please . . ."

"THEN COME OUT! NOW!"

Good. I had them right where I wanted them. It was time to turn up the heat and really show them who was boss. "Please, please, please, please, please, please . . ."

"ALL RIGHT," the voice shouted. "WE GET THE IDEA!"

But this was no time for mercy. I went after

them with everything I had. "Please, please, please, please, please, please . . ."

"ALL RIGHT, YOU WIN, YOU WIN! JUST STOP THAT AWFUL BEGGING AND COME OUT!"

Smiling at my victory, I raised my hands and started for the open door.

The open door with the bright light blazing through it.

The bright light that blinded me so I didn't see my brother's science project in front of me.

The science project with the huge wheelbarrow full of porcupine quills.

The science project with the huge wheelbarrow full of porcupine quills that—Oh, forget it. Let's just cut to the

"WHOA!"
K-RASH
"YEOW!"
rattle-rattle-rattle

disaster.

You seasoned *My Life As . . .* readers have no doubt figured out what the "WHOA!"-ing, *K-RASH*ing, and "YEOW!"-ing are all about.

But the *rattle, rattle, rattl*ing? Got you there,

didn't I? No biggie, just me fighting to get out of the quill-filled wheelbarrow full of quills. (You think that's a tongue twister, just wait eight sentences.)

The only problem was the sticky glue.

The sticky glue that was still all over me.

The sticky glue that was still all over me and drying.

The sticky glue that was still all over me and—

(I'm doing it again, aren't I? Sorry.)

The point is . . . **I WAS COVERED IN POINTS!** About a thousand of them! In fact, every quill that my supersticky body stupidly touched stuck to my stupidly supersticky body. (Hey, I warned you it was coming.)

By the time I crawled out of the wheelbarrow, I was covered from head to foot in porcupine quills.

Unfortunately, that was the good news.

The bad news was, when I staggered to my feet and stepped out of the door to meet the group, about a billion people freaked.

"What is it?!" they gasped.

"It's the alien!" someone screamed.

"Without his disguise!" others shrieked.

"It's not true!" I yelled. "I'm no alien. I knew all that stuff on the test because I cheated!" I waved my quill-coated arms, trying to get them to understand—which only caused more gasps, screams, shrieks, and the ever-popular

Thud-Thud-Thud

which, of course, is the sound of freaked-out neighbors hitting the ground as they pass out.

"No!" I cried as I continued toward them.

More gasps, screams, shrieks, and

*Thud-Thud-Thudd*ing.

"Quick, get the tranquilizer gun!" one of the F.I.B. agents shouted.

"Got it!" another yelled.

"Not a tranquilizer gun!" I shouted.

"Relax, the dart will just put you to sleep so you don't zap us with any of your fancy-schmancy, alien death-rays."

"I don't want to go back to sleep! I was passed out through most of the last chapter!"

"So?"

"So, whose name do you see on the cover? Shouldn't I be awake through *some* of the story?"

"Don't listen to him!" the other agent shouted. "He's just trying to confuse you with his alien author talk."

"I'm telling the truth!" I cried as I stumbled toward the light. "I'm an honest person."

"So you *didn't* cheat on that test! So you really are an alien!"

"No, I mean, yes, I mean—"

"Ready . . . ," the first agent shouted.

"It's me!" I cried. "Wally McDoogle!"

"Aim . . ."

And then, just before they opened fire (and we had to change this title to *My Life As a Human Dartboard*), a white van squealed around the corner, blasting its horn.

Everyone turned as it raced toward us. Suddenly, it veered to the right, and bounced over the curb onto our lawn.

"LOOK OUT!" people screamed as they leaped to the side.

HONK! HONK! it honked as it headed straight for me.

"AUGH! AUGH!" I *augh*ed as I was about to die. (Hey, you try coming up with something clever to yell when you're getting ready to croak.)

And then, just when I was about to become the van's permanent hood ornament, it slammed on its brakes.

SCREECH! the brakes screeched.

"WHEW!" the people whewed.

FAINT! I fainted.

Oh, and there was one other sound I forgot to mention: "YOU GUYS ARE RUINING MY LAWN! YOU GUYS ARE RUINING MY LAWN!" (That, of course, would be Dad—racing out the front door, showing his fatherly concern.)

But the fun and games weren't over yet. Before I knew it (which is pretty easy since I'd already passed out), a big guy in a ski mask threw open the van door, ran to me, and scooped me into his arms.

"WHAT ARE YOU DOING?!" the F.I.B. agent shouted.

"We're from 'Save Our Lovely Pluto Pals'!" the big lug shouted. Then, before anybody could stop him (or figure out which mental hospital he'd escaped from), he raced to the van, threw me in the back, and hopped in behind the wheel.

A woman in another ski mask shrieked from the passenger seat, "Hurry up, you nincompoop! Hurry!"

"You needn't shout so," Big Lug whined as he began

*grind-grind-grind*ing

the gearshift, looking for first gear. "Just because I am large does not mean I am insensitive."

As I woke up, the voices seemed familiar, but I couldn't place them.

"HURRY!" the passenger screamed.

To which Big Lug replied, "Please, you are disturbing my

grind-grind-grind

inner peace."

The passenger cried, "You'll be a lot more disturbed than that if they throw us back in prison!"

Where had I heard those voices?

By now, all sorts of lights were shining into the van. All sorts of tanks had aimed their cannons at us. And all sorts of soldiers were marching toward us.

But that was small potatoes, compared to the real threat.

BANG BANG BANG BANG

We gave a start and spun around to see Dad pounding on the van's side window and shouting, "Get this hunk of junk off my lawn before I call the cops!" (Which wouldn't be hard, since every cop in the state was standing beside him.)

"You'd better do what he says," I called from

the back. "My dad's pretty touchy about his lawn."

"That is what I

grind-grind-grind

am attempting. However,

grind-grind-grind

I am unable to find the appropriate—"

. . . *mmoOOOOORAV*

That did it. He found a gear and we started off! Unfortunately, it wasn't the right gear, which explains the . . . *mmoOOOOORAV* instead of the *VAROOOOOomm*. . . . That's right, Big Lug had not found FORWARD, but REVERSE. Which was okay, except for the part about

*K-rash*ing

into the F.I.B. cars and

*K-areen*ing

into the crowd, and our tires doing even more

dig-dig-digg-ing

into the—

"YOU'RE RUINING MY LAWN! YOU'RE RUINING MY LAWN!"

And, if that wasn't enough chaos, there was always the shrieking passenger. "What are you doing!?! You've got us in REVERSE!!"

"Oh, really?" Big Lug pouted. "Perhaps that's why I cannot see where we are—"

"LOOK OUT!"

K-Snap
K-WOOOOOSH

"—going."

I looked out the back and saw we had just snapped off a fire hydrant as the water *K-wooooshed* a hundred feet into the air.

What was it about these people that seemed so familiar? (Not only did I recognize the voices, but also the lack of driving skills.)

"Who are you?" I shouted.

"We're from **S.L.O.P.P.**," the woman cried.

"**S.L.O.P.P.**?" I yelled.

"Yes! **S**ave **O**ur **L**ovely **P**luto **P**als."

"But I'm not from Pluto!"

"It's okay, young Pluto Pal," Big Lug said as he swerved and

HONKKKK

barely missed a giant semitruck. "You don't have to lie to anyone anymore."

"But—"

The woman shouted, "We at **S.L.O.P.P.** know the prejudice you are facing."

"That is correct," Big Lug agreed. "Which is why we formed **S**ave **O**ur **L**ovely **P**luto **P**als in the first place."

"But . . . that doesn't spell **S.L.O.P.P.**," I cried. "You've got the **L** and the **O** mixed up."

"Well, what do you expect?" Big Lug complained. "We're ecological revolutionists, not English teachers."

Suddenly, I knew why I recognized the voices, and the dimwitted intelligence, and the bad

SQUEAL
HONK-HONK

driving.

"Wait a minute!" I shouted. "Didn't you guys used to have a different name?"

"Why, that is correct, young Pluto Pal. Before we were sent to prison, we had an entirely different cause."

"Which was . . . ?" I asked, already fearing the worst.

"Snails." Big Lug beamed. "We used to be **S.O.S.** . . . **S**ave **O**ur **S**nails."

"We were world-famous," the woman bragged. "Some brat even wrote a couple of books about us called—"

"My Life As Dinosaur Dental Floss?" I asked.

"That's one!" Big Lug cried in excitement. "You've heard of it?"

"Uh, yeah." I swallowed nervously. "And the other one was . . . *My Life As a Walrus Whoopee Cushion?"*

"Did you hear that, Dear?" Big Lug grinned. "They've read about us all the way to Pluto!"

"Doesn't surprise me," the woman said. "We were heroes . . . till that creepy author kid got us thrown in jail . . . *twice*."

"Yes, his actions were definitely not appreciated. Although my last stay in jail certainly improved my speaking skills."

"It makes no difference." The woman sneered. "He better hope he never sees us again!"

Big Lug agreed. "We would definitely do his body some major harm." Then, being the thought-

ful, sensitive type, he turned to me and said,
"But that's enough talk about him. Why don't
you tell us a little bit about

K-rash
tinkle-tinkle-tinkle
(Kiss that street lamp good-bye.)

yourself, little Pluto Pal?"

Chapter 5

Photo Op

So there we were—the crazy revolutionists—driving backward down the street at night just like, well, just like crazy revolutionists driving backward down the street at night . . . while Yours Truly was

SCREECH
roll-roll-roll
SLAM!

bouncing around in the back of their van like a human

SCREECH
roll-roll-roll
SLAM!

pinball.

Big Lug had just asked me to tell them about
my life on Pluto, and now they waited for the
details. The way I figured it, I had two choices:

1. Tell the revolutionists who I really was so
   they could majorly hurt me.
2. Tell the revolutionists who I really wasn't
   so our pursuers could majorly hurt me.

Decisions, decisions.

But instead of answering, I followed in the
steps of all great political leaders . . . I completely
dodged the question and made up another.
"Excuse me?" I asked.

SCREECH

"You wouldn't happen to know where we're—

roll-roll-roll
SLAM!

going, would you?"

"The zoo," the lady answered.

"The zoo?" I cried. "Isn't that where Wally
McDoogle released all the animals and they
went on a wild rampage?"

"That's right," she said.

"And isn't that where you went crazy and finally got arrested?"

"Yes." Big Lug sighed dreamily. "It does hold some fond memories for us."

"That's why we're meeting some kid reporter there," the lady explained.

"A reporter?!" I asked.

SCREECH

"That's right," she said. "Some girl has promised to videotape our story and sell it to *59½ Minutes*."

"Not only that"—Big Lug grinned—"but she's only charging us—

roll-roll-roll

$24.95."

SLAM!

"Wait a minute," I said, getting a little suspicious (not to mention a lot bruised). "A reporter is charging *you*?"

"That is correct."

"Did she happen to give you a name?"

"There she is now!" Big Lug cried as he hit the

SCREEEEEEECH

brakes, and I hit the

K-Bamb

front seat.

The good news was, we were done playing Wally Ping-Pong Ball. The bad news was, when they opened the door, pulled me out of the van, and dragged me in front of the video camera, I immediately recognized the girl behind the camera.

"We're still talking $24.95?" the ski mask woman asked.

"Plus expenses," the girl said.

Only this was no ordinary girl.

"Expenses?" Big Lug asked.

Unfortunately, she was anything but ordinary.

"Yeah. It will cost you another $24.95 for me to actually press the camera's ON button—"

This was the girl dedicated to making her first million off me before she turned fourteen.

"—and another $24.95 to make sure I point the camera in the right direction—"

That's right. This was—who else?—my best friend. The one, the only . . .

"—and another $24.95 to keep my finger *on*
the RECORD button."

. . . Wall Street!

Of course, I wanted to call to her for help
(after all, that's what best friends are for). But I
knew better than to come between her and
making money—especially when it involved
little incidental things . . . **LIKE SAVING MY
LIFE!** (I'm shouting again. Sorry.)

I suppose I could give her the benefit of the
doubt. You know, actually believe she would
come to my rescue. Believe she would give up
all that money. I suppose I could also believe in
fairies (since the odds are more in Tinkerbell's
favor than Wall Street's), but I don't.

In any case, they finally finished their nego-
tiations. Of course, the money Wall Street asked
for was outrageous. So, being as good a busi-
nessman as he is a driver, Big Lug gave the perfect answer:

"Do you want cash or Master Charge?"

But before Wall Street could respond, the
F.I.B. cars roared around the corner and raced
down the road.

"Quick!" the woman cried, "let's get out of
here!"

"An excellent suggestion," Big Lug agreed.

The two of them spun around, ran for the

zoo's fence, and hopped over it. A moment later they were disappearing into the night.

"Whew"—I sighed—"that was close."

"Not as close as this will be," Wall Street said as a dozen cars slid to a stop all around us. Then, just like old times, my friend with the bullhorn (and bad math skills) climbed out of his car and shouted:

"STEP AWAY FROM THE PORCUPINE, MISS!"

"Porcupine?" Wall Street asked. "Where?"

"THE ONE YOU'RE STANDING BESIDE!"

She turned to me and burst out laughing. "This is no porcupine. This is my friend, Wally McDoogle."

"ARE YOU SURE? BECAUSE HE LOOKS JUST LIKE THE CREATURE WE HAD SUR-ROUNDED IN TOWN."

Again Wall Street laughed. "Of course it's Wally." Turning to me, she said, "Show them you're Wally, Wally."

I grinned and said, "No sweat." I took a single step forward and immediately

K-trip
K-fall
K-flopp-ed

over a crack in the sidewalk.

"See?" Wall Street shouted. "Who else but Wally McDoogle could be such a klutz?"

"YES, I SEE YOUR POINT," Bullhorn Man sadly agreed.

"Thanks," I said to Wall Street as I staggered back to my feet.

"No problem, but it'll cost you."

"Just charge it to my account," I said.

"I always do."

I smiled. Good ol' Wall Street . . . full of love, good thoughts, and friendship to the very end.

"THAT'S TOO BAD," Bullhorn Man said as he started back toward his car. "BECAUSE WE'RE OFFERING A $1,000 REWARD FOR ANY PORCUPINES FROM PLUTO."

"Oh, *that* porcupine," Wall Street suddenly shouted. "Well, now that you mention it, this *is* him! Yes, he's attacking me as we speak!" (Good ol' Wall Street . . . full of greed, greed, and even more greed to the very end.)

Instantly, she grabbed my hand and started hitting herself over the head with it. *"HELP ME!"* she shouted. *"AH! AH! HELP ME! HELP ME!"*

It was awful. Terrible. Some of the worst acting I'd seen in my entire life. (Her friendship wasn't so hot, either.)

But it did the trick. Suddenly, a dozen tranquilizer guns appeared from the various cars, each and every one preparing to send me into snoozeville.

Mr. Bullhorn shouted: "UNHAND THAT CHILD, YOU MEAN PLUTONIAN!"

"Wall Street," I cried as she continued hitting her head with my hand, "what are you doing?"

"Trust me," she whispered.

Now I *knew* I was in trouble.

She turned to the agents and cried, *"OH, MY, THAT HURTS. HE'S SUCH A BRUTE!"*

"Wall Street," I whispered, "they're going to tranquilize me and take me off to some lab, where they'll run experiments on me for the rest of my life!"

"I know, but—*OH, STOP, I'M BEGGING YOU!*—we're talking a thousand—*OH, OH, OUCH, OUCH!*—bucks."

"We're also talking my life!"

"I'll—*OH, WHO WILL SAVE ME?!*—split the money with you."

"You will?"

"Sure, the usual—*HE IS SUCH A MON-STER!*—$990 bucks for me, $10 for—*I FEEL SO FAINT!*—you."

"But—"

"Plus an additional $11 to me for—*WON'T SOMEBODY TRANQUILIZE THIS AWFUL MONSTER?!*—postage and handling."

"But, but—"

"Which means you'll only owe me—*WON'T SOME BIG F.I.B. HERO SAVE ME?*—one dollar."

"OKAY, PEOPLE!" Bullhorn Man shouted.

"But, but, but—"

"TAKE YOUR POSITIONS!"

The way I figured it, I had two choices:

1. Stick around and continue my *but-but-but* motorboat imitation while becoming the U.S. government's science fair project for the next eighty years—

"READY . . ."

2. Or pretend to be a prickly porcupine from Pluto and escape into the zoo.

"AIM . . ."

So, since I really hate getting shots, especially a dozen of them at a time, I turned from Wall Street toward the fence—

"OH, MY! HE'S HEADING FOR THE ZOO!"

—and followed my revolutionist buddies.

"FIRE!"

Chapter 6

Hide and Go FREAK!

I raced to the zoo's fence and leaped over it. Well, I almost leaped over it. Unfortunately, my leaper was a little lame, unluckily landing me on my lower lumbar.

Translation: I fell on my . . .

K-OAFF!

rear.

No problem, I'd just get up, try another leap, and do another . . .

K-OAFF!

Look, it's not like I'm not athletic. I go to the gym all the time. Yes sir, nothing beats a good 45-minute workout of trying to tie my gym shoe laces. Don't laugh, I'm getting pretty good at it.

With practice maybe someday I'll even work my way up to those laces with the heavy metal tips on the ends! (Hey, everybody needs a goal in life.)

In the meantime, all I had to do was

K-OAFF!

climb over the fence.

The good news was, the F.I.B. agents were laughing so hard they couldn't aim their tranquilizer guns, so they kept missing me and hitting

K-zing—K-Pop
woooosh
(There goes the van's tire.)

everything else around them.

K-zing—K-Rash
tinkle-tinkle-tinkle
(There goes another streetlight.)

And not only things, but people, too.

K-zing—K-Stick

"Hey, I'm Wall Street. You're not suupp-poooozZzzzzzz ... *snore* ..."

I watched as my friend slowly slumped to the street and drifted into nighty-night land.

Now I was on my own.

Now I'd have no help from my friend.

(Now I might actually be able to escape without owing her a bazillion dollars.)

Quicker than you can say, "Ah, come on, those F.I.B. guys aren't that bad of a shot. . . . And, by the way, what does F.I.B. stand for?" I raced back to Wall Street and, amid all of their

*K-zing, K-zing, K-zing*ing,

I pulled her into the van.

Then, quicker than I can say, "F.I.B. means Federal Investigator Boys, and really, they are that bad of a shot, at least when they're laughing. And, besides, whatever darts hit me bounced off my quills, so be sure to wear quills the next time you go to the doctor for a vaccination." Anyway, quicker than I can say all of that, I turned the van's key, tromped on the accelerator, and

*. . . mmoOOOOORAV*ed

off.

But, as you already noticed, the van was still in REVERSE, which explains the

SQUEEEAL
"LOOK OUT! HE'S GOING TO
KILL US ALL!"

and the

*K-RASH*ing

through the zoo's fence, with plenty more

*K-zing, K-zing, K-zing*ing

thrown in for good measure.

The good news was, we escaped the F.I.B.

The bad news was, we didn't escape the zoo's
gift shop, which was

SQUEEEAL
"AHHHH!"
K-RASH

straight ahead.

(And you thought we were going to land in a
polar bear pit or something, didn't you? Honestly,
what type of moron do you take me for? Don't
answer that!)

Unfortunately, there was no time for tricks
of wit with polar bear pit bits. Say that seven

times fast. Go ahead, I'll wait. (That's what you get for calling people morons.)

Anyway, there was no time for polar bear pit bits (you're getting good at that) when I was busy crashing into the gift shop and rolling to a stop right in front of a display case full of animal noses.

A DISPLAY CASE FULL OF ANIMAL NOSES?!

Relax, they were all fake—you know, the type you wear as jokes . . . little piggy noses, lion noses, elephant noses?

Suddenly, I had a brainstorm. Actually, in my case, it's more like a brain squall . . . no, make that a brain tropical depression. The point is, since I still couldn't remove the quills (they were stuck to me harder than the gum under our cafeteria tables), maybe I could disguise myself so the F.I.B., and the **S.L.O.P.P.**s, and even Wall Street wouldn't recognize me.

So, with that bit of minimal brain activity, I crawled out of the van and limped toward the counter. Unfortunately, my lack of driving skills had not only put a giant hole through the gift shop's wall, but had also set off the automatic sprinklers.

So, as the automatic sprinklers began to automatically sprinkle, the slippery floor caused me to automatically

"WHOA!"
Slip
K-thud.

And, if that wasn't bad enough, the all-too-familiar blinding lights blazed through the wall's hole, followed by a voice that was even more all-too-familiarer:

"THIS IS THE F.I.B. COME OUT WITH YOUR CLAWS UP!"

(Doesn't that guy ever get laryngitis?)

I ducked down behind the counter. I reached into the display case, grabbed the nearest piggy nose, and plunked down $3.95 for it. (Hey, I might be an escaped suspect, a revolutionists' hostage, a porcupine from Pluto, a terrible driver, and, and, all right, I'll say it, and a *cheater on science tests,* but I'm no thief!)

I put on the nose and quickly stood up, shouting, "There's nobody here but us piggies!"

The F.I.B. wasted little time replying with their usual:

K-zing, K-zing, K-zing.

Now, as much as I wanted to stick around and talk about old times, maybe share the latest photos of my little aliens back home, I knew it was time to leave. It was time to make like Dad's old slacks when he squeezed into them for my cousin's wedding and . . . *split.*

I spun around and saw a door directly behind me. On it was a tiny little sign that read:

Zookeeper's Office

What luck! He must have moved his office here while they were rebuilding the one I had destroyed. (Or he was trying to keep his location hidden in case I ever returned for a visit.)

Either way, I crawled to the door, carefully opened it, and slipped inside. I was in the midst of some very familiar surroundings. The office was identical to his old office. Yes sir, there were the same ol' shelves I'd crashed into, with the same ol' books I'd knocked off onto the same ol' computer that had shorted out and opened up all the animal cages. Such wonderful memories . . .

Unfortunately, there were a couple of other memories in the room that weren't so wonderful . . . like one very big Big Lug and his female partner! That's right. There were my old buddies standing near the open window they'd crawled through. At the moment, they were bending over the computer, staring at the monitor.

"What's going on?" I whispered.

They spun around and exclaimed, "Pluto Pal!"

"What are you doing?" I asked as I rose to my feet.

"We're going to free all of your cousins," the woman said.

"My cousins?"

"That is correct." Big Lug beamed. "Aardvarks, armadillos, platypuses—you name them, we're going to save them. It shouldn't just be porcupines from Pluto. We should be saving all of God's weirder-looking critters!"

"But—"

"We know this computer can do it," the woman said as she leaned over the keyboard. "This was how that wretched Wally McDoogle freed all the animals the last time we were here."

Big Lug nodded. "We're just not sure how his sinister little mind figured it out."

I swallowed nervously. "Maybe he didn't do it on purpose. Maybe it was an accident."

They both looked at me. "An accident?"

I nodded. "Maybe he just accidentally knocked down those books from that shelf above it."

"These books here?" Big Lug asked, pointing to the wrong shelf.

"No," I said, walking toward him. At least I wanted to walk toward him. Unfortunately,

walking involves certain coordination skills I
tend to lack, which explains my

*stumble, stumble, stumbl*ing.

It would also explain my trying to catch
myself by reaching up and grabbing—what
else?—the right bookshelf.

Which would also explain the

*Thud-Thud-Thudd*ing

of the books as they fell directly from the shelf
and onto the

K-rackle, K-sizzle, K-pop

computer.

Yes sir, it was just like old times with . . .

- The computer shorting out.

- The cage doors unlocking.

- And two **S.L.O.P.P.**s jumping up and down
  in excitement.

"Yes!" the woman screamed in joy.
"Our hero!" Big Lug shrieked in gratitude.

Such love and appreciation. I tell you, it doesn't get any better than that. Well, except for the

K-zing, K-zing, K-zing

of tranquilizer darts shooting through the open window. And the

"OUCH!"

of one finally making its way through my quill coat, sticking into my rear, and sending me fast to sleep.

Other than that, things were just greaaatzzzzz. . . .

Chapter 7

Stranger-er and Weirder-er

The nice thing about going unconscious so many times in one book is that it gives you plenty of time to dream. And if you just happen to be working on a superhero story, dreaming means you don't have to carry around that bulky ol' laptop computer. Instead, all you have to do is sort of close your eyes and . . .

When we last left our supergood good guy, he was being hypnotized by our superbad bad guy's Hypno-beam. That's right, he was about to spend the rest of his life in front of the TV, becoming as useless as a toothbrush at a denture convention, or Wall Street at a charity auction, or our author trying to play any sport whatsoever.

"Hey, I heard that!" (Worse than that, I just dreamed it.)

Then, as luck would have it, along with some incredibly cool story-telling on this author's part—

"Yeah, right."

—our hero accidentally sits on the remote control, which accidentally changes channels to the presidential debates.

And why the presidential debates, you ask? (You are asking, right? Good.)

Suddenly, he is watching something so boring that viewers actually get bored of the boredom of being bored. And that's when it hits him:

"Hey, I'm bored!"

(Told you.)

Using all of his superstrength, he manages to pull his eyes away. And, although he sprains an eyeball or two in the process, he breaks the beam's power over him. Now he will do something more meaningful with his life like—

"Play video games?"

No. Even more meaningful.

"What could be more meaningful than scoring 100,000,000 points on 'Creepy Crypt-Robbers from Cleveland'?"

"Wait a minute, who keeps interrupting?"

"Just me—Couch Potato Dude. I've got nothing else to do in this section of the story."

"Well hang on, I'll get to you in a second."

"Hope so."
Anyway, our heroically handsome hero decides to try something super-swell, awesomely awesome, and excitingly exciting, like...

SAVE THE WORLD!

"Nice print size," Couch Potato interrupts. "But I would have added some hero music, too."

"Do you mind?"

"Sorry."
Instantly, he reaches down to his

Gadgetron Belt (sold at superhero
stores everywhere) and presses the
button that changes his body into
electricity. Now he can enter the
cable at the back of his TV set.

"Wait a minute, he can't do that!"
Potato Dude cries.

"I'm Invento Man. I can do anything
I imagine."

"Yeah, but——"

"It's not like I sit around and
watch TV all day. I use my imagination and think up things."

"Excuse me," the author interrupts. "Are you
guys done?"

"Sorry."
Without further interruption,
Invento Man shoots through the cable
all the way to Couch Potato's secret
broadcast studio. From there our hero
leaps out of the TV monitor and mate-
rializes before Couch Potato.

"I still think that's cheating,"
our bad buddy broods.

"I'm the good guy; good guys don't
cheat."

"I'm not talking about you, I'm talking about our author."

"He doesn't cheat, either."

"Didn't you hear how he got into this whole porcupine mess? Haven't you been reading his story?"

"Guys!"

"I would have if you hadn't hypnotized me with your Hypno-beam."

"Well, you really haven't missed much, except the part where the F.I.B. agents tranquilized him and——"

"GUYS!! We'll get back to my story in just a minute. Right now, it's time for your fight scene."

"Are we there already?" Invento Man asks.

"Just about. But first, Couch Potato has a line."

"I do? Oh, right. Thanks."

Suddenly, our bad boy lets out a menacing

"Boo-hoo-hoo-ha-ha-ha!"

and shouts, "Your ignorant intelligence
is no match for me, Midget Mind!"
    "Hey, how come he gets all the
cool lines?" Invento Man asks.

"Because you get all the cool gadgets."

    "But even your cool gadgets won't
stop me from destroying everyone's
imaginations!" Couch Potato cries.
    "They won't?"
    "That's right, because soon I'll
drain what little imagination is left
from TV and invent programs where you
just sit around and watch other
people sit around and talk."
    "Oh, you mean TV talk shows?"
Invento Man says.
    "What? They've already been in-
vented?"
    "Yup."
    "Okay, but what about TV shows
where you just sit around and watch
everyday people do everyday things?"
    "We call that 'Reality TV.'"
    "No way."

"Sorry."

Growing more and more desperate, Couch Potato Dude cries, "All right! Instead of shows with a few commercials, I'll make shows that are entirely commercials!"

"'Infomercials,'—yup, got them, too."

"Alack and forsooth! I am aghast and agog!"

"What does all that mean?"

"It's Shakespeare. He always used it in big speeches like I'm about to make."

"Cool. Go for it."

"Woe is me! I am ruined! I am wrecked. What shall I do? Where shall I turn? Oh, what, pray tell, does life's fickle finger forecast for my future?"

"Well...there's always our fight scene."

"Hey, that's right. We still haven't gotten to it."

"And you still have that dreaded Hypno-beam, which, believe me, really is your best weapon for controlling the world."

"You think so?" Couch Potato asks, turning to the giant Hypno-beam machine across the room.

"You bet. In fact, it looks like you've only got it turned up to *'Control Freak.'* And the way I see it, you can crank that puppy all the way up to *'Total World Domination.'*"

"Except Cleveland," Dude adds.

"Why do you keep bringing up Cleveland?"

"It keeps getting laughs."

"All right, the beam will even control Cleveland!"

"So what am I waiting for?!"

"Got me."

Suddenly, without a word ('cause there's been way too many words in this scene already), the terrifying television tyrant tiptoes to his Hypno-beam machine, grabs the dial, and cranks it all the way up to—

"Wally . . ."

—and cranks it all the way up to—

"Wally, wake up. Wally, wake up and say something to the camera."

My eyes fluttered open.

The good news was, I was coming to and leaving my strange superhero story behind.

The bad news was, I was coming to, leaving my strange superhero story behind . . . and entering my even stranger reality.

A reality that involved me riding on the back of a convertible in some sort of parade. But this was no ordinary parade. (How could it be in one of these books?) Instead of marching bands playing out of tune, or goofy clowns riding tiny tricycles, or little girls dropping batons, we were heading down Main Street surrounded by weird people riding weird floats and holding weird signs. Like the folks just ahead of us. They rode a float and carried a sign that read:

D.I.P.S.

while, all the time, shouting, "**D**own with **I**nsulting **P**oisonous **S**nakes! They have feelings, too! **D**own with **I**nsulting **P**oisonous **S**nakes!"

I shook my head, not believing what I was seeing and hearing. I turned around and saw another float behind us. On it were people carrying a sign that read:

J.E.R.K.S.

as they shouted, "**J**ustice **E**ntitles **R**ats to **K**indness and **S**afety! **J**ustice **E**ntitles **R**ats to **K**indness and **S**afety!"

And directly behind them were my ol' revolutionist pals carrying their

S.L.O.P.P.

sign and shouting—what else?—"**S**ave **O**ur **L**ovely **P**luto **P**als! **S**ave **O**ur **L**ovely **P**luto **P**als!"

I reached out to the driver in the front seat and tapped him on the shoulder. "Excuse me!" I shouted. "Excuse me, what's going on?"

The driver turned and, to my horror, I saw it was my older brother Burt (or was it Brock?)! But my horror wasn't because he was driving (though that's certainly scary enough). It was because he didn't recognize me!

"Oh, Mr. Pluto Pal," he said, "I'm so glad you're awake. What can I do for you?"

"Brock? (Or is it Burt?)," I said. "Don't you recognize me?"

"Of course, Mr. Pluto Pal. And I just want to say it's such an honor to be your driver."

"What??"

"You might find this interesting, but I'm actually doing a science project on porcupines. And when my brother's friend Wall Street here—" He motioned to the girl in the passenger's seat beside him. "When she asked me to drive you, well, I jumped at the chance."

Wall Street turned to me. She held the video camera to her eye and was obviously taping. "Isn't this cool?" she shouted.

I would have liked to agree calmly. Instead, I screamed hysterically: "WHAT'S GOING ON?!"

"You're a celebrity!" she said.

"Me? What did I do?"

"You mean besides visiting us from Pluto?"

I glanced down at my arms. They were still covered in quills. "Oh, no." I groaned.

"Oh, yes!" She beamed. "But that's just the beginning!"

"What else?"

"Thanks to my fast thinking (along with little details like **S.L.O.P.P.**s rescuing you from the F.I.B.), I've made you into someone all the weirdo groups in the nation are rallying behind."

"What?!"

"That's right. By freeing those zoo animals, you've become the hero and spokesperson for all the nut-case causes in the country!"

"You're not serious?"

"Not only am I serious, I'm making millions by signing you up for television endorsements."

"Television endorsements?"

"You name it, we're selling it. I've even gotten us a TV movie deal, which I'm filming as we speak!"

"Wall Street!"

"Excuse us!" someone shouted. I turned to a group of folks running toward the car. "We're from the group **We Help Ants and Cockroaches be**K**ause of Our Stupidity**," the leader shouted.

"Oh, the **W.H.A.C.K.O.S.**," Wall Street said.

"Yes. Sorry we're late. Where do you want us in the parade?"

Wall Street glanced down at the clipboard beside her. "Let's see . . . you're right behind the **Let Our Slugs Enjoy Relaxing Saunas**, which are right after the **Institute for Nonviolence between Squirrels And Nuts Etc.**"

"Thanks!" he shouted as his group took off to join the parade.

"Now," Wall Street said as she turned back to me, "where were we?"

"**Endorsements and craziness and TV movies!**" I shouted.

"Right." She nodded. "Oh, here's one of our actors now."

I spun around to see Junior Whiz Kid, the seven-year-old brainiac from some of my earlier adventures.

"Mr. Pluto Pal!" he shouted. "Mr. Pluto Pal!"

"What are you talking about?" I cried. "It's me, Wally McDoogle! Remember? We met in *My Life As a Tarantula Toe Tickler!*"

"Just play along," Wall Street whispered from behind the camera.

I turned to her. "What??"

"Just play along. I've paid him as an actor."

"A what??"

She stopped looking through the camera and sighed. "All right, let's try it again. Places, please."

Junior Whiz Kid took a few steps back.

Wall Street looked back into the camera and shouted, "And . . . action!"

Once again, Junior ran up to the car, shouting, "Mr. Pluto Pal, Mr. Pluto Pal!"

"Uh . . . what?" I said, not exactly sure of my lines.

"I have constructed . . . your rocket to the exact . . . specifications that . . . you . . . required. . . ."

"My what?!"

"You . . . know . . . ," he said, "the . . . rocket . . . to return . . . you . . . to Pluto."

Now, I don't want to be mean, but there was only one person in the world whose acting was worse than his.

"Oh, . . . ," I said, ". . . *that* . . . roc . . . ket. . . ."

(You guessed it. Harrison Ford could relax. I was no threat to his career.)

"Yes"—Whiz Kid nodded—"*that* . . . rocket."

Luckily, before we could continue our Academy Award–winning performances, my brother hit the

SQUEEEAL

brakes.

"What's going on?!" Wall Street shouted at him as she turned off the camera. "You ruined a perfectly good take!"

But instead of answering, Brock (or was it Burt?) pointed straight ahead.

There, directly in front of us, were a half-dozen guys in yellow biohazard suits right out of some Steven Spielberg movie. Beside them were a bunch of yapping dogs.

I glanced over at Wall Street. By the surprised look on her face, I guessed these were not more of her paid actors.

And by the way they suddenly were rushing the car, waving nets and stun guns, and shouting, "STOP HIM! DON'T LET HIM ESCAPE!" I suspected they really weren't interested in getting my autograph, either.

Chapter 8

The Not-So-Great Escape

Call me a little oversensitive, but there's something about a half-dozen guys in biohazard suits with electric gizmos and barking dogs that makes me feel, oh, I don't know . . . A LITTLE SCARED TO DEATH! So I did what any scared-to-death chicken (or porcupine) would do. I leaped from the car and waddled for my life! (I would have run, but you try running with a million quills poking your legs!)

Unfortunately, the bio-boys and their

"Bark! Bark! Bark!"-ing

buddies stayed right on my tail.

Unfortunatelier (don't try that word on your English teacher), all my little weird pals from all their little weird groups saw my problem and offered to help.

"Over here!" the president of **L**et **O**ur **S**lugs **E**njoy **R**elaxing **S**aunas yelled. He motioned me toward his float. "Over here!"

Like a fool, I ran to his float and he helped me aboard.

Then we headed to the giant sauna that was the centerpiece of their float. "In here!" he shouted as he opened the door. "Hide in here!"

Luckily, this wasn't those rat guys' float (I really hate rats, don't you?), so I took his advice and stepped inside.

Well, I wanted to step. But it's hard stepping when the entire floor is covered in . . .

Slip . . . "WHOA!"
K-Splat
Slip . . . "WHOA!"
K-Splat

. . . slugs!

That's right, and after a dozen or so more *Slip*s, "WHOA!"s and *K-Splat*s, I was covered from quill to quill in slippery, sticky (Repeat after me—"EEEwwwwww!" Very good.) slug slime.

Of course, the **L.O.S.E.R.S.** started shouting, "You're killing our slugs! You're killing our slugs!"

So, as much as I wanted to stick around, I knew it was time to

Slip . . . "WHOA!"
K-Splat

move on. I slipped (literally) out the back and
leaped off the float.

"There he is!" my bio-suit buds shouted.

Luckily, someone else was also shouting.
"Over here, Pluto Pal! Over here!"

Up ahead I saw the next float—the one
belonging to the **W**e **H**elp **A**nts and **C**ockroaches
be**K**ause of **O**ur **S**tupidity.

The good news was, the **W.H.A.C.K.O.S.**
didn't have rats, either.

The bad news was, they had a bazillion ants
and cockroaches scampering around inside a
giant display case.

And what's so bad about that, you ask. (Is
this your first *My Life As* . . . book or something?) Let me explain . . .

It's bad news when they help me onto their
float and my feet are still slick with slug slime,
which causes me to

"WHOA!"
Sliiiiiiiide . . .
K-rash

into their giant display case!

Not a big problem, except for the part about my completely destroying the display case and sending every type of ant and cockroach you can imagine (and some you don't want to) flying into the air.

Luckily, they didn't fly far.

Unluckily, it was because they all landed on

piift piift piift piift
piift piift piift piift

me.

And, since I was still covered in sticky slug slime, they not only landed on me . . . they stuck on me!

That's right. The creepy crawlies were the perfect accessory to my quill-and-slime wardrobe. And the fact that they were all

*twitch twitch twitch*ing
*twitch twitch twitch*ing

gave a certain "life" to my ensemble. (And you thought the slug slime was gross.)

But, my stroll down Creepmare Lane wasn't quite over.

Next stop . . . the **I.N.S.A.N.E.**s—those crazies with all the squirrels and nuts. (At least they weren't rats; I really do hate rats.) Of all the floats in the parade, theirs was the cutest. Unfortunately, the key word here was . . . *was*.

Was as in it *was* cute . . . until I slammed into its side and knocked down their little nut tree display.

Was as in it *was* cute . . . until the little nut tree display fell into the not-so-little squirrel cage.

Was as in there was suddenly a huge herd of squirrels running all over the place . . . and a gazillion nuts rolling all over the street.

Unfortunately, the nuts weren't the only things rolling. Because nothing takes your mind off *slipp*ing, *stick*ing, and, yes, *twitch*ing like a good case of Rollerblading. Only, instead of blades, you have a gazillion little round nuts under your—

"Whoaaa!"
"Waaaaa!"
"Wheeeee!"

feet.

The bad news was, the bio-suit boys were still after me. "Don't let him get—

"Wheeeee!"

"Waaaaa!"
"Whoaaa!"

—away!"

The badder news was, the next stop on my little tour of "Let's Destroy Wally's Life" was a visit to the folks from **J**ustice **E**ntitles **R**ats to **K**indness and **S**afety.

But instead of letting me near their float (which is the same as letting me destroy their float), their president opened a nearby manhole cover and shouted, "In here, Porcupine Pal! In here!"

So, with nothing else better to do than roll for my life, I

"Whoaaa!"-ed
"Waaaaa!"-ed and
"Wheeeee!"-ed

myself toward the open manhole until I

"AUGHHHHHHHHHHH!"

dropped out of

K-splash

sight.

When I bobbed to the surface, I looked around. The place was majorly dark—blacker than the hamburgers my little sister charburned for dinner last night.

"Are you okay?" the **J.E.R.K.S.** president shouted from up above.

"Yeah!" I yelled as I splashed about. "But it sure is creepy down here by myself!"

"Don't worry about that!" he shouted.

"What do you mean?"

But instead of an answer, I heard about a hundred little

*k-splash, k-splunk, k-sploosh*es

all around me.

"What's that?" I shouted. "What are you doing?"

"We're sending you down some company!"

"Company?" I yelled, suddenly fearing the worst.

"That's right!" he shouted. "We're sending you down all of our favorite

k-sploosh, k-splunk, k-splash

rats!"

Ever have one of those days?

(Unfortunately, I have one of those lives!)

And, as much as I appreciated their kindness and the thoughtful parting gifts, I knew it was time to swim for my life (or what was left of it)! I swam through that storm drain for all I was worth—($1.92 if you count the spare change in my pocket, which came to, oh, I don't know, $1.92).

Eventually, I saw an opening.

Eventuallier (there's another not-to-use word), I shot out of the pipe

"AHHHHHHHH!"

and landed in a nearby

K-splash

stream.

"THERE HE IS! AFTER HIM!"

I looked over my shoulder. A couple of my bio-suit buds and one of their pet barkers were already standing on the roadway waiting for me. And, to make things more interesting, they'd called in a helicopter or two.

(I just love surprise parties, don't you?)

I quickly swam to the stream's bank with my usual gasping, choking, and coughing up of a lung or two. Then I staggered to my feet and started to run.

The good news was, the water had washed off all my insect pals as well as most of the slime.

The bad news was, it had *not* washed off my quills.

And the badder news was, they'd set up a net trap for me. You know the type I'm talking about—a net hidden on the floor of the woods. The type just waiting for some unsuspecting porcupine to step into it and

"WHOOOAAA!"
"AHHHHHHHH!"
dangle-dangle-dangle-dangle.

That's right, before I knew it, I was suddenly posing for the cover of some weird, goofy kid's book, wearing my best porcupine quills and pig nose.

And, crowding forward to get their faces into the photo (not to mention their captured prey into their clutches) were my bio-suit buds and their pet

"YAP! YAP! YAP!"-per.

Chapter 9

Goin' Home

So there I was hanging from the tree like some human piñata. Only instead of knocking me down with sticks, the fellows in the bio-suits were thinking more along the lines of electric stun guns or, if I was lucky, the ever-popular, and always fashionable, tranquilizer darts that I'd grown so fond of.

Fortunately, they didn't have the chance to use either.

Unfortunately, it was because someone or something wanted me even more.

zzzz . . . ZZZZ . . . ZZZZ . . . ZZZZ

"What's that noise?" Bio-suit #1 shouted as he looked into the air.

"I don't know," Bio-suit #2 cried. "It sounds like—"

Suddenly, a light brighter than what the cops use to pull my brother over for speeding blared down on us.

Suddenlier still, their howler hound dog started howling.

And for good reason. This light did not belong to the F.I.B. It didn't even belong to the helicopter circling above us. Instead, it belonged to a voice that bellowed:

"THIS IS PLUTO PAL'S MOTHER SHIP! STEP BACK FROM THAT ALIEN, OR WE WILL HAVE TO DISINTEGRATE YOU WITH OUR DESTRUCTO BEAM!"

"Oh, no!" Bio-suit #1 shouted. "It's Pluto Pal's mother ship!"

"And if we don't step back," Bio-suit #2 cried, "they'll disintegrate us with their Destructo Beam!"

(I tell you, if these guys were any dimmer, my mom could use them as night-lights in our hallway.)

In an incredible act of courage, both men turned from the light and bravely raced out of the woods for all they were worth, with the barking bow-wower right behind.

This left only me to confront the invaders.

Only me to be the hero and boldly defend my planet.

Only me to turn to face the light and bravely shout:

"Don't hurt me! I'll do whatever you want! Please, please, please, please—"

"Wally."

"—please, please, please—"

"Wally!"

"—please, please, please . . ." (Don't laugh, I think I was wearing them down. Now, where was I? Oh, yeah.) "Please, please, please . . ."

"KNOCK IT OFF, ALREADY!"

I came to a stop—not because I'd finished my argument; I still had a good twenty or thirty pleases left in me—but because the invaders sounded a little irritable. And since I am allergic to being Destructo-Beamed, I decided to pause a moment.

"Wally, it's me, Wall Street!"

I looked up into the light. "What??"

"Yeah," the voice shouted. "And Junior Whiz Kid, too. Hang on, we're coming down!"

They turned off the light, and I could see the two of them floating toward the ground. They stood on a small, saucer-shaped hovercraft. You know the type I mean . . . like what your friends build in their spare time . . . if they just happen to have the IQ of a supercomputer . . . and if their name happens to be Junior Whiz Kid.

"All right!" I shouted in excitement. My friends were here! They'd come for me! All my troubles were over!

(Well, two out of three wasn't bad.)

In a matter of seconds, they landed and hopped off the hovercraft. Then, with a hatchet, Junior started

*hack hack hack*ing

away on the rope that held me in the air until I finally

"AUGH!"
K-Thud

fell to the ground.

That was the good news.

The bad new was, Wall Street was videotaping it and didn't like the way it looked through her camera.

"Cut, cut, cut!" she cried. "All right, let's try it again!"

"Guys, wait a min—"

Despite my protests they hauled me back up into the net and—

"Action!"

—hacked away at the net until I fell—

"AUGH!"
K-Thud

—down again.
"Cut, cut, cut! That's still not right. Let's try it again, please!"
"But, guys—"
"Action!"

"AUGH!"
K-Thud

By the time they finally "saved me" (after fifteen or sixteen takes), I was so dazed and semiconscious that I didn't know where we were going.

Which was actually a good thing, considering where we *were* going.

All I remember was getting dumped onto the hovercraft.

K-Bamb!

"Be careful, that's his head."
"Sorry."
"That'zzz all righttt. . . ." I grinned idiotically. "It'zz haard to feeeel paaaain whennn youu'reee loozzzzing conzzziouzzz . . ."
"Good," Junior said as we

ZZZZ ... ZZZZ ... ZZZZ ... zzzz

rose into the sky. "It is quite encouraging to hear you say that you are not concerned with pain."

"Why'zzz thaaat?" I said as I continued drifting off into la-la land.

"Because when we arrive at my laboratory, strap you to my rocket ship, and send you to Pluto, you won't feel a thing."

"That'zzz nizzzz. I liiike rocketzz shipzzzz . . ."

* * * * *

On the Wally Weirdness Scale of 1 to 10, the dream I had rated around a 12.5. In it I was bent, folded, and stuffed inside the nose cone of a tiny rocket ship. I mean, I was jammed tighter than my cousin's size 12 body into her size 8 wedding gown.

Outside, somebody (who sounded a lot like Wall Street) shouted, "Light the fuse!"

And somebody else (who sounded a lot like Junior) shouted, "Fuse ignited!"

Then somebody who sounded a lot like me shouted, "Excuse me! Excuse me!" (I would have shouted louder, but it's hard shouting with your kneecap halfway down your throat.) Then there's the matter of all those quills "Ow!" still stuck to my kneecap.

"Not now, Wally," Wall Street yelled as she started counting down: "TEN . . . NINE . . ."

"What's going on?!"

"We're launching you into outer space," Junior Whiz Kid explained.

"Outer space!"

". . . EIGHT . . ."

"Just for a while. Until they think you're heading back home."

"Oh." I sighed. "Good thing this is a dream; otherwise, I'd be pretty freaked."

"This is no dream," Junior said.

"Right." I chuckled, "That's what they always say in dreams."

". . . SEVEN . . ."

Before Junior could argue, I heard another familiar and comforting voice. "THIS IS THE F.I.B.! THROW OUT THAT ALIEN AND COME OUT WITH YOUR HANDS UP!"

Like I said, I just love reunions. Who knows, maybe the bio-suit boys would also show up, along with their puppies, and my pals from **S.L.O.P.P.**, and everyone else (well, except for those rats).

". . . SIX . . ."

But before I had a chance to order a cake or

even set up the tripod for a group picture, there
was a loud

K-BAMB!

that sounded an awful lot like the *K-Bamb*s of
laboratory doors being blown off their hinges.
This, of course, was followed by the *pitter-patter*
of army tanks, and a thousand or two National
Guard troops rushing in.

"... FIVE ..."

"What's going on! I can't see. Let me out of here! Let me out!"

"You hear something, Sergeant?" one of the
soldiers called.

"It's coming from that rocket with the burn-
ing fuse."

"Oh, you mean this one that's pointed out
the window?"

"Let me out! Let me out!" I began moving, forcing the
rocket to wobble back and forth.

"Look at that, Sarge. The rocket not only
talks, it walks."

"Let me out. Let me out!"

"Amazing. What they won't think of next."

"... FOUR ..."

With one last push, I finally managed to tip
over the rocket. It slammed onto the ground,
and I

K-POPed

out of the nose cone.

"Look at that, Sarge," the soldier called, "the rocket just gave birth."

Only then did I realize that Junior was right. This was no dream. How could it be? I could never dream up such mentally challenged characters, let alone such stupid dialogue.

". . . THREE . . ."

That's when I knew it was time to get out of there. It was time to make another not-so-great escape. Time to use all of my athletic skills and

K-Thud

trip over my shoelaces.

"Look at that, Sarge, the baby is almost as clumsy as that Wally McDoogle kid."

Actually, the tripping wasn't so bad. The embarrassing part was getting up and stagger-ing into the window blinds (complete with win-dow blind cords). Then, of course, there was the mandatory fighting with those cords . . . which led to the obligatory getting tangled up in them . . .

". . . TWO . . ."

. . . which led to my stumbling back against the rocket ship . . . which, of course, led to getting all of those cords (and all of myself) wrapped around the fin of the rocket ship.

". . . ONE . . ."

I was hoping someone would untie me, but everybody was too busy enjoying the show (which would explain the wild applause and standing ovation).

Unfortunately, before I could take a bow and start an encore, Wall Street finished her verbal math skills:

". . . ZERO . . ."

Suddenly, I went from the calf-tying Wally event to broncobusting the rocket. Yes sir, it was just like a rodeo. Well, except for the part about being strapped to a rocket . . . that pointed out a window . . . that

*K-WOOOOOSH*ed

off as I

"AHHHHHHHH!"-ed

my lungs out.

Other than that, it was nearly identical.

Chapter 10

Wrapping Up

My minor flight was majorly fantastic . . . though I could have done with some peanuts. And that in-flight movie they were showing? The one with my life flashing before my eyes? Just a little too scary for my tastes.

But the view was terrific . . . until all my kicking, squirming, and

"AUGHHHHHHHH!"-ing

threw us off course. So, instead of flying to Pluto, I and my little rocket fellow shot straight up into the air, then did a bunch of loop-the—

"Whoaaa!"
"Waaaaa!"
"Wheeeee!"

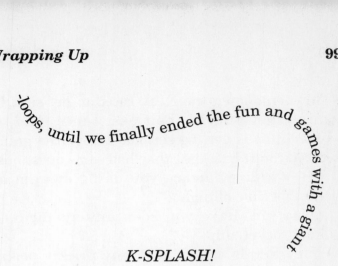

-loops, until we finally ended the fun and games with a giant

K-SPLASH!

into the ocean.

The good news was, the impact was so great that it ripped the pig nose right off my face. (It almost ripped my face off my face.)

The gooder news (sorry about the English) was, the salt water started dissolving all the glue that held all those quills to me.

And the goodest news (I'm realier sorrier) was, by the time I finally swam to the beach and did my minimum daily requirements of

*choke, choke, choke*ing,
*gasp, gasp, gasp*ing,
and
*hurl, hurl, hurl*ing,

the quills had all fallen off.

Moments later, the F.I.B. raced to my side. Of course, they offered their assistance. And, of courser (this is getting serious, I hope the grammar cops don't bust me), they had some questions:

"Hey kid, what are you doing swimming alone this time of night?"

"Hey kid, have you seen any suspicious-looking rocket ships?"

"Hey kid, have you seen any prickly porcupines riding those rocket ships?"

Looking up into their faces, I knew I could lie. After all, my pig nose was gone and all the quills were washed off. But, at that moment, I realized lying was just as dishonest as cheating. And if there's one thing I'd learned about cheating, it was that it might look like you're winning, but you're actually taking the longer and more painful scenic route to becoming a loser.

So, with a heavy sigh, and the realization that I'd be grounded until the twenty-third century, I opened my mouth and started practicing something I hadn't practiced for the last twenty-four hours . . .

Honesty.

When we last left our story, Couch Potato was just about to turn his

Hypno-beam all the way up to Total
World Domination, when Invento Man
decided to use his cool imagination
to stop him.

But instead of leaping at the dan-
gerously destructive dude and beginning the typical end-of-the-story
fight (you know, the part where they
go crashing to the floor and start

*Roll-Roll-Roll*ing

to one side of the room and then

Roll-Roll-Rolling

to the other, all the time shouting
and grunting, while being careful not
to use bad language)...

Instead of all that stuff, our
hero reaches into his back pocket,
pulls out the latest book he's been
reading (something about Crocodiles
and Junk Food, or is it Humans and
Hairballs?) and flings it at our
felonious foe. It bounces off his
noggin and falls to the floor.

Glancing down at it, the bad boy

bruiser shouts, "What is this? A new superhero weapon?"

"No way." Invento Man laughs. "It's something we call...a book."

"A book?" Couch Potato asks as he scoops it up and opens it. "Kind of a stupid weapon, isn't it? I barely felt it hit my head."

"It's not for the outside of your head," our hero explains as he begins to approach. "It's for the *inside*."

"Inside?"

"Yes, by reading it, you'll experience all sorts of action and adventure. You'll meet all sorts of cool people and visit places and——"

"You mean like TV."

"No, it's a thousand times better than TV because *you* get to do all the imagining."

Da-da-la-la-dee-dee...

"Wait a minute, is that 'wrap-up music' I'm hearing?"

"Yeah, we better hurry."

Couch Potato looks back at the book, then flips through the pages, frowning. "But it's just a bunch of words. There're no pictures or nothin'."

"Exactly. The words are like sparks to set your imagination on fire. And your imagination is a thousand times more interesting than looking at pictures or a TV screen. It's like *you* get to create your own TV shows and movies inside your own head. Not only do you get to create them, you get to act in them and everything!"

"Whoa, that *is* cool!"

"Cooler than controlling the world?"

"Sure. This way I can imagine even bigger things—like being supreme dictator of the galaxy."

"Including Cleveland?"

"Yes, including Cleveland! Say, you got any more of these 'book' thingies?"

"Yup, there're tons of them at the library and at bookstores. Want me to show you?"

"Wow, that would just be so super-swell!"

"All right!"

And so, as the music grows louder

Da-da-la-la-dee-dee...

and the credits begin to roll, our two
new friends throw their arms around
each other and head off into the sunset, searching for more books that
will set their imaginations on fire.

"Yeah," Couch Potato says, "maybe
we'll even find one whose ending
isn't as sappy as this one."

Invento Man nods. "This was pretty
bad, wasn't it?"

"Hey! I heard that!" the author writes. "Come
back here and apologize."

"Sorry." Potato Dude shrugs. "We're
done with the story."

"You can't leave my story without getting my
permission!"

"Actually," Invento Man explains,
"you've already got us heading off
into the sunset."

"Listen, if you don't turn around and come back, you can just forget about me giving you blond hair for your next superhero story."

"Who says we're going to be in your next story?" Couch Potato asks.

"Good point," Invento Man agrees. "I hear the author Billy Myers is looking for new characters."

"Is he?" Couch Potato asks.

"Oh, yeah. And so is William Myers and Bill Myers."

"Cool."

"Guys!"

"So let's hurry to the library and read how those authors end their books."

"Guys . . . Guys . . ."

But it is no use. The two friends head off to start reading—as they prepare to use their God-given imagination to create characters and adventures greater than any TV or

movie...or maybe even this superhero
story.

I paused to look down at Ol' Betsy's screen.
My characters were right. It was kind of a
sappy ending. But it was also pretty honest.
And right now, for me, being honest was a real
big thing. *Real Big.* Even though it meant:

- Flunking my science test (which drops my
  semester grade to somewhere around a
  G–). But that's okay, Mr. Reptenson
  promises if I work real hard I might be
  able to get it up to an F. And that's not
  even counting the extra credit I can earn
  by passing out umbrellas before he speaks
  and mopping up the floor when he's done.

- Then there's the little problem about all
  the damage I did at the zoo . . . again. No
  biggie. Mr. Zookeeper is holding no
  grudges. In fact, as soon as he gets out of
  the mental hospital (there's something
  about my name that makes his face vio-
  lently twitch—but that's okay, the medica-
  tion seems to be helping). . . . Anyway, as
  soon as he gets out, he promises I can
  work to pay off the damages. I'm not sure

of the details, but it will involve something like hand-feeding the polar bears, flossing the alligators' teeth, and running around the gorilla cage dressed up like a banana. Sure glad he's not holding a grudge.

• And, finally, there's all the damage I did around the house—like destroying Burt's (or is it Brock's?) science project. Unfortunately, my brother is still searching for me. Fortunately, Dad has agreed to protect me from him. Even though I've completely ruined his lawn, Dad has put twenty locks all over my bedroom door. Talk about being cool and not holding a grudge. (Though I would feel a little better if he'd let me out at least once a month . . . and if he hadn't threatened to take the entire family on vacation to Disney World, if so much as one hair on my head was damaged.) Still, it was a thoughtful gesture . . . I think.

Warning, Wally. Warning, Wally.
Warning, Wally. Warning, Wally.

My cell phone began ringing with that special ring telling me it was Wall Street.

Ringing with that special ring telling me that, whatever I do, don't be a fool, don't be a moron, don't pick up. But, with those options, what other choice did I have?

"Hey, Wall Street," I answered after I popped open the phone.

"Wally, I just heard from your **F**riends **O**utreach **O**nly to **L**eeches **S**ociety."

I frowned. "Never heard of them."

"They used to be **S.L.O.P.P.**"

I shifted nervously. "Oh, them."

"They're still on the run from the F.I.B. But they promised to pay us one million dollars in cold, hard cash if you turn yourself over to them."

"Turn myself over to those two?" I croaked. "Why?"

"So they can express their appreciation to you for completely ruining their lives again."

"Oh."

She continued. "It would be the usual split."

I nodded. "$999,990 for you, $10 for me?"

"Plus that additional $11 to me for postage and handling."

"Right. Listen," I said, "I'd like to help, but there are a whole lot of other people who want to show their 'appreciation' to me first."

"Like who?"

"Like my brother, like the zookeeper, like my dad—"

"Yeah, but nobody's offering this type of money!"

"I know, but . . . well, it just wouldn't be honest to let them crowd in front of the others just because they have money. I mean, isn't that sort of like cheating?"

"So?"

"So, if there's one thing I've learned, it's that cheating doesn't pay."

"But—"

There was a knock on the door.

I covered the phone. "Who is it?"

"It's Mom, Sweetheart. Time to go feed those polar bears."

"Be right there." I turned back to the phone. "Sorry, Wall Street. Maybe some other time."

"But, but—"

"Gotta go," I said. "But if you can think up another plan that doesn't involve cheating, let me know."

"But, but, but—"

I let her continue her motorboat imitation and hung up. I knew I had done the right thing, the honest thing. Because if there's one thing I'd learned, it's that honesty really is the best policy.

"Oh, and Honey, don't forget the dental floss."

It might not be the easiest thing, or even the least painful—

"I've already got your banana costume in the car. Let's go!"

—but it is always . . . the best.

You'll want to read them all.

THE INCREDIBLE WORLDS OF WALLY McDOOGLE

#1—My Life As a Smashed Burrito with Extra Hot Sauce

Twelve-year-old Wally—the "Walking Disaster Area"—is forced to stand up to Camp Wahkah Wahkah's number one all-American bad guy. One hilarious mishap follows another until, fighting together for their very lives, Wally learns the need for even his worst enemy to receive Jesus Christ. (ISBN 0-8499-3402-8)

#2—My Life As Alien Monster Bait

"Hollyweird" comes to Middletown! Wally's a superstar! A movie company has chosen our hero to be eaten by their mechanical "Mutant from Mars"! It's a close race as to which will consume Wally first—the disaster-plagued special effects "monster" or his own out-of-control pride—until he learns the cost of true friendship and of God's command for humility. (ISBN 0-8499-3403-6)

#3—My Life As a Broken Bungee Cord

A hot-air balloon race! What could be more fun? Then again, we're talking about Wally McDoogle, the "Human Catastrophe." Calamity builds on calamity until, with his life on the line, Wally learns what it means to FULLY put his trust in God. (ISBN 0-8499-3404-4)

#4—My Life As Crocodile Junk Food

Wally visits missionary friends in the South American rain forest. Here he stumbles onto a whole new set of impossible predicaments . . . until he understands the need and joy of sharing Jesus Christ with others. (ISBN 0-8499-3405-2)

#5—My Life As Dinosaur Dental Floss

A practical joke snowballs into near disaster. After prehistoric-size mishaps and a talk with the President, Wally learns that honesty really is the best policy. (ISBN 0-8499-3537-7)

#6—My Life As a Torpedo Test Target

Wally uncovers the mysterious secrets of a sunken submarine. As dreams of fame and glory increase, so do the famous McDoogle mishaps. Besides hostile sea creatures, hostile pirates, and hostile Wally McDoogle clumsiness, there is the war against his own greed and selfishness. It isn't until Wally finds himself on a wild ride atop a misguided torpedo that he realizes the source of true greatness. (ISBN 0-8499-3538-5)

#7—My Life As a Human Hockey Puck

Look out . . . Wally McDoogle turns athlete! Jealousy and envy drive Wally from one hilarious calamity to another until, as the team's mascot, he learns humility while suddenly being thrown in to play goalie for the Middletown Super Chickens!
(ISBN 0-8499-3601-2)

#8—My Life As an Afterthought Astronaut

"Just 'cause I didn't follow the rules doesn't make it my fault that the Space Shuttle almost crashed. Well, okay, maybe it was sort of my fault. But not the part when Pilot O'Brien was spacewalking and I accidentally knocked him halfway to Jupiter. . . ." So begins another hilarious Wally McDoogle MISadventure as our boy blunder stows aboard the Space Shuttle and learns the importance of: Obeying the Rules! (ISBN 0-8499-3602-0)

#9—My Life As Reindeer Road Kill

Santa on an out-of-control four wheeler? Electrical Rudolph on the rampage? Nothing unusual, just Wally McDoogle doing some last-minute Christmas shopping . . . FOR GOD! Our boy blunder dreams that an angel has invited him to a birthday party for Jesus. Chaos and comedy follow as he turns the town upside down looking for the perfect gift, until he finally bumbles his way into the real reason for the season. (ISBN 0-8499-3866-X)

#10—My Life As a Toasted Time Traveler

Wally travels back from the future to warn himself of an upcoming accident. But before he knows it, there are more Wallys running around than even Wally himself can handle. Catastrophes reach an all-time high as Wally tries to out-think God and rewrite history. (ISBN 0-8499-3867-8)

#11—My Life As Polluted Pond Scum

This laugh-filled Wally disaster includes: a monster lurking in the depths of a mysterious lake . . . a glowing figure with powers to summon the creature to the shore . . . and one Wally McDoogle, who reluctantly stumbles upon the truth. Wally's entire town is in danger. He must race against the clock and his own fears and learn to trust God before he has any chance of saving the day. (ISBN 0-8499-3875-9)

#12—My Life As a Bigfoot Breath Mint

Wally gets his big break to star with his uncle Max in the famous Fantasmo World stunt show. Unlike his father, whom Wally secretly suspects to be a major loser, Uncle Max is everything Wally longs to be . . . or so it appears. But Wally soon discovers the truth and learns who the real hero is in his life. (ISBN 0-8499-3876-7)

#13—My Life As a Blundering Ballerina

Wally agrees to switch places with Wall Street. Everyone is in on the act as the two try to survive seventy-two hours in each other's shoes and learn the importance of respecting other people. (ISBN 0-8499-4022-2)

#14—My Life As a Screaming Skydiver

Master of mayhem Wally turns a game of laser tag into international espionage. From the Swiss Alps to the African plains, Agent 00½th bumblingly employs such top-secret gizmos as rocket-powered toilet paper, exploding dental floss, and the ever-popular transformer tacos to stop the dreaded and super secret . . . Giggle Gun. (ISBN 0-8499-4023-0)

#15—My Life As a Human Hairball

When Wally and Wall Street visit a local laboratory, they are accidentally miniaturized and swallowed by some unknown stranger. It is a race against the clock as they fly through various parts of the body in a desperate search for a way out while learning how wonderfully we're made. (ISBN 0-8499-4024-9)

#16—My Life As a Walrus Whoopee Cushion

Wally and his buddies, Opera and Wall Street, win the Gazillion Dollar Lotto! Everything is great, until they realize they lost the ticket at the zoo! Add some bungling bad guys, a zoo break-in, the release of all the animals, a SWAT team or two . . . and you have the usual McDoogle mayhem as Wally learns the dangers of greed. (ISBN 0-8499-4025-7)

#17—My Life As a Computer Cockroach
(formerly *My Life As a Mixed-Up Millennium Bug*)

When Wally accidentally fries the circuits of Ol' Betsy, his beloved laptop computer, suddenly whatever he types turns into reality! At 11:59, New Year's Eve, Wally tries retyping the truth into his computer—which shorts out every other computer in the world. By midnight, the entire universe has credited Wally's mishap to the MILLENNIUM BUG! Panic, chaos, and hilarity start the new century, thanks to our beloved boy blunder. (ISBN 0-8499-4026-5)

#18—My Life As a Beat-Up Basketball Backboard

Ricko Slicko's Advertising Agency claims that they can turn the dorkiest human in the world into the most popular. And who better to prove this than our boy blunder, Wally McDoogle! Soon he has his own TV series and fans wearing glasses just like his. But when he tries to be a star athlete for his school basketball team, Wally finally learns that being popular isn't all it's cut out to be. (ISBN 0-8499-4027-3)

#19—My Life As a Cowboy Cowpie

Once again our part-time hero and full-time walking disaster area finds himself smack-dab in another misadventure. This time it's full of dude-ranch disasters, bungling broncobusters, and the world's biggest cow—well, let's just say it's not a pretty picture (or a pleasant-smelling one). Through it all, Wally learns the dangers of seeking revenge. (ISBN 0-8499-5990-X)

#20—My Life As Invisible Intestines

When Wally becomes invisible, he can do whatever he wants, like humiliating bullies, or helping the local football team win. But the fun is short-lived when everyone from a crazy ghostbuster to the *591/2 Minutes* TV show to the neighbor's new dog begin pursuing him. Soon Wally is stumbling through another incredible disaster . . . until he finally learns that cheating and taking shortcuts in life are not all they're cracked up to be and that honesty really is the best policy. (ISBN 0-8499-5991-8)

#21—My Life As a Skysurfing Skateboarder

Our boy blunder finds himself participating in the Skateboard Championship of the Universe. (It would be "of the World," except for the one kid who claims to be from Jupiter—a likely story, in spite of his two heads and seven arms.) Amid the incredible chaotic chaos by incurably corrupt competitors (say that five times fast), Wally learns there is more to life than winning. (ISBN 0-8499-5592-6)

#22—My Life As a Tarantula Toe Tickler

Trying to be more independent, Wally hides a minor mistake. But minor mistakes lead to major mishaps! Soon Wally begins working for Junior Genius (the boy super-inventor from book #21), and becomes a human guinea pig to backfiring experiments such as Tina, the giggling tarantula whom he accidentally grows to the size of a small house. Now, our boy blunder must save Tina, his life, and the entire city. Through all of this, Wally learns the importance of admitting mistakes, taking responsibility for his own actions, and always telling the truth. (ISBN 0-8499-5993-4)

#23—My Life As a Prickly Porcupine from Pluto

It's just a little cheating on a little test. There's nothing wrong with that, right? WRONG! So begins another McDoogle disaster as one lie leads to a bigger lie and a bigger lie and even a bigger lie. Soon the entire world believes Wally is an outer-space alien (who looks like a giant porcupine) trying to take over the planet. He is pursued by tanks, helicopters, even a guided missile or two—not to mention his old friends at S.O.S. (Save Our Snails) who, unfortunately, are now trying to save him! It is another hair-raising (er, make that quill-raising) misadventure as our boy blunder learns that honesty really is the best policy. (ISBN 0-8499-5994-2)

MEET WALLY McDOOGLE'S COUSIN

Trouble (and we're talking BIG trouble) runs in Wally's family. Follow his younger cousin Secret Agent Bernie Dingledorf and his trusty dog, Splat, as they try to save the world from the most amazing and hilarious events.

SECRET AGENT DINGLEDORF

. . . and his trusty dog, SPLAT 🐾

BY BILL MYERS

1—*The Case of the Giggling Geeks*

The world's smartest people can't stop laughing. Is this the work of the crazy criminal Dr. Chuckles? Only Secret Agent Dingledorf (the country's greatest agent, even if he is only ten years old) can find out. Together, with supercool inventions (that always backfire), major mix-ups (that become major mishaps), and the help of Splat the Wonder-dud, er, Wonder-dog, our hero winds up saving the day . . . while discovering the importance of respecting and loving others. (ISBN: 1-4003-0094-0)

2—*The Case of the Chewable Worms*

The earth is being invaded by worms! They're everywhere . . . crawling on kids' toothbrushes, squirming in their sandwiches, making guest appearances in Mom's spaghetti dinner. And, worst of all, people find them . . . tasty! But is it really an invasion or the work of B.A.D.D. (Bungling Agents

Dedicated to Destruction)? Only Secret Agent Dingledorf and his trusty dog, Splat, can find out and save the day . . . while also realizing the importance of doing good and helping others.
(ISBN: 1-4003-0095-9)

3—*The Case of the Flying Toenails*

It started out with just one little lie. But now, everybody is coming down with the dreaded disease—Priscilla, parents, even Super-dud, er, Super-dog, Splat. They go to bed perfectly normal one night, then wake up the next morning with jet-powered toenails! Who knows the truth behind this awful sickness? Who can stop it? Only Secret Agent Dingledorf and his not-so-trusty (at least in this book) sidekick, Splat, can find the cure and save the day . . . while discovering how important it is to be honest and always tell the truth.
(ISBN: 1-4003-0096-7)

4—*The Case of the Drooling Dinosaurs*

What's going on? Why are there dinosaurs slobbering all over the city? Is this the work of Dr. Rebellion, the man who hates following the rules? Only Secret Agent Dingledorf and his trusty dog, Splat, can find the answer. Only they can save the day . . . while also learning the importance of obeying those in charge. This funny, zany story is an adventure about following rules—and the chaos that happens when we don't!
(ISBN: 1-4003-0177-7)

5—*The Case of the Hiccupping Ears*

The boys at B.A.D.D. (Bungling Agents Dedicated to Destruction) are at it again. This time they are out to confuse the entire world. People who are exposed to their awful

Brain Wave Mixer Upper suddenly forget the right way to eat, see, talk, hear, smell, and even walk! Only Secret Agent Dingledorf and his trusty dog, Splat, can save the day . . . while learning how wonderfully God has made the human body! (ISBN: 1-4003-0178-5)

6—*The Case of the Yodeling Turtles*

Everybody's pets are going crazy. Cats think they can sing opera. Dogs think they're country western stars. Even Priscilla's turtles think they can yodel. Is this another plan to take over the world by B.A.D.D. (Bungling Agents Dedicated to Destruction)? Only Secret Agent Dingledorf can save the day (along with his trusty dog, Splat—when Splat's not too busy signing autographs) . . . while he learns the importance of treating pets and animals with kindness. (ISBN: 1-4003-0179-3)